BOOK TWO

GOOD CROOKS

Dog Gone!

Mary Amato

Illustrated by **Ward Jenkins**

MINNEAPOLIS

First published by Egmont USA in 2014

Darby Creek
A division of Lerner Publishing Group, Inc.
241 First Avenue North
Minneapolis, MN 55401 USA

For reading levels and more information, look up this title at www.lernerbooks.com.

Library of Congress Cataloging-in-Publication Data

Amato, Mary.
    Dog gone! / by Mary Amato ; illustrated by Ward Jenkins.
      pages cm. — (Good crooks ; book two)
    Summary: When their thieving parents steal a rich and famous dog,
  twins Jillian and Billy, who have grown tired of being crooks, must find a
  way to get Poochie Smoochie back to her owner. Includes activities.
    ISBN 978-1-60684-397-0 (hardcover)
    ISBN 978-1-60684-510-3 (digest pbk)
    ISBN 978-1-60684-404-5 (eBook)
    [1. Conduct of life—Fiction. 2. Robbers and outlaws—Fiction.
  3. Brothers and sisters—Fiction. 4. Twins—Fiction. 5. Family life—
  Fiction.] I. Jenkins, Ward, illustrator. II. Title.
  PZ7.A49165Dog 2014
  Fic]—dc23   2013018297

Manufactured in United States of America
2-44626-20849-7/20/2017

BOOK TWO

GOOD CROOKS

Dog Gone!

Don't miss

Book One of *Good Crooks*

"... will have beginning readers eager for more ..."
—*Publishers Weekly*

Contents

1 The Whopper... 1

2 Bake and Burp 12

3 Hip to the Hop 18

4 Punked... 26

5 Oodles of Poodles 33

6 Diary of a Wimpy Dog 40

7 Poochie Smoochie.................................51

8 What's Worse than Worst?..................... 59

9 Midnight Madness................................. 71

10 Choo Choo Uh-Oh.................................. 78

11 It's a Bird. It's a Plane. It's a Burger?... 89

12 *Tip Tip Squish* 103

Secret Extras 115

1

The Whopper

I woke up early because two birds flew in my window and tap-danced on my head. Just kidding.

I woke up early because a squirrel slid down our chimney and ate my pillow. Just kidding again.

I woke up early because a rhino rang our doorbell and asked if he could use our bathroom. Just kidding even more.

You want to know the truth? I

don't know why I woke up early. I just opened my eyes and wiggled my toes. Then I snuggled back under my covers.

It was a school day. Mom and Dad would want me and my sister, Jillian, to sleep late, eat junk food, and then go out and steal stuff. In other words, they would want us to be crooks like them. That's the Crook way.

If you read my first book, you've

already met the Crook family. If not, let me explain. My parents, Ron and Tanya Crook, are famous crooks. They want me and Jillian to follow in their footsteps.

Mom and Dad like to start the day by closing their eyes and imagining which store to rob. So I closed my eyes and imagined breaking into the grocery store and stealing all the bacon.

Then I imagined the owners coming in to work and seeing that they'd been robbed. They started to cry big, fat tears. I got all choked up. See, here's my big secret: I don't want to rob anybody. I'm a nice guy.

That's a big problem! My parents would be mad if they found out that their little boy was turning out to be nice.

There was only one person I could talk to: my twin sister, Jillian. We both have big feet, big ears, freckles, and a crazy desire to do good deeds.

I hopped out of bed and tiptoed down to the kitchen. *Tip. Tip. Tip.*

I peeked in. Jillian was working on her computer. She always wakes up early.

I pulled up a chair. "Jillian, I . . . I . . . I want to—" I wasn't sure what

I wanted to do. I only knew what I
didn't want to do. I didn't want to rob
anybody.

She looked at me.

"Jillian, I . . . I . . . I want to—"

She moved back. "Billy, are you
going to barf on me?"

"No. I'm not sick," I whispered.
"I want to do a good deed today, but I
don't know what to do."

Her eyes grew big. "I have an idea," she whispered. She reached into her back pocket and pulled out a piece of paper. "Look at this flyer! It came in the mail yesterday, and I've been thinking about it ever since."

PLEASE HELP THE
LUCKY DOG SHELTER

MAKE MY DAY!
Donate money
Have a bake sale or a yard sale
Donate dog food or treats
Or give a dog a loving home

Help us keep our dogs healthy and happy!

"See?" Jillian whispered. "The dog shelter doesn't have enough money for food or medicine."

I looked at the picture of the cute dog. "We should help," I said.

"Shhh," Jillian said. "We can't let Mom and Dad hear us talking like this!"

I thought about those cute dogs, and my heart started to go all gooey in the center. I imagined Jillian and me rolling into the Lucky Dog Shelter with food and toys and medicine. The dogs would be so happy. I imagined the whole celebration:

Huskies high-fiving!

Dalmations dancing!

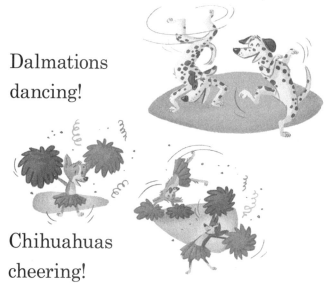

Chihuahuas cheering!

Basset hounds bunny-hopping!

A warm, happy feeling filled me. Oh, the joy of helping others!

I turned to Jillian. "We're insane. This is so *not* the Crook way."

"We're not insane. We're just

different from Mom and Dad," Jillian whispered. "Let's donate a whole pile of money." She leaned in. "Let's go honest. Let's earn it."

A totally mad crazy idea.

"I'm in," I said.

"Let's have a bake sale," Jillian said. "We could make cupcakes and sell them in the park."

I started jumping up and down. Cupcakes do that to me.

Jillian grinned. "Okay, get dressed first so we're ready to go. Then meet me back here in the kitchen."

We tiptoed up to our bedrooms. If you're a Crook, you can never leave the house without a disguise. So I put on my stockings, my wig, my best dress, and my glasses.

My Mrs. Whiffbacon disguise.

Who wouldn't buy cupcakes from a nice old lady?

I looked in the mirror. Hmm. Mrs. Whiffbacon needed something fresh.

A fake foam rear end, of course!

Everyone should have fake rear ends. I have five.

The Gumball.

The Board. →

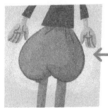The Beanbag.

The Square →

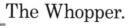The Whopper.

Mrs. Whiffbacon deserves the very biggest, so I put on the Whopper and covered it with my best dress. Then I looked in the mirror and gave my rear end a shake. It would be very embarrassing to go out without a proper-looking rear end.

"Yo, Whiffbacon, how's it shaking today?" I asked myself.

I looked shocked and said in my old lady voice: "Young man! Please call me Mrs. Whiffbacon!"

Mrs. Whiffbacon is a pain in the rear sometimes.

I grabbed my purse and ran downstairs as fast as my big bottom would allow.

2

Bake and Burp

Mrs. Sippy was waiting in the kitchen.

Who is Mrs. Sippy? My sister's favorite disguise!

"Fancy meeting you here, Mrs. Sippy," I said in my old lady voice. "Your hair is looking especially gray today."

"Good morning, Mrs. Whiffbacon," my sister said in her old lady voice. "Your rear end is looking especially big today."

"It's a big bottom, but it's a happy bottom!" I said.

"Let's get to work," she said, pulling some eggs out of the fridge. "We need to make a bunch of cupcakes to sell."

"What are we going to tell Mom and Dad?" I whispered.

"Ron and Tanya Crook always sleep late. We can be done and back before they even wake up," she said.

I put on an apron and started cracking eggs into a bowl.

"Billy, wait!" Jillian opened up her laptop. "Let's find a recipe."

"I don't need no stinking recipe," I said.

Jillian used a recipe. I used my brain. That's how I roll.

Jillian put cherries and coconut in hers. What did I put in mine? Toothpaste and dead ants. Just kidding. Chalk and chili peppers. Just kidding. Oatmeal and bacon. Not kidding. Seriously. Dude, everything tastes better with bacon.

We mixed and whipped and poured and put those babies in the oven.

"While we're waiting for the cupcakes to bake," Jillian said, "let's make some signs." She got paper and markers.

Here's how her sign turned out:

Here's how mine turned out:

Ding! Finally, the cupcakes were done!

Here's how hers turned out:

Here's how mine turned out:

You can't be good at everything.

I got two sodas out of the fridge and handed her one. "Hey, Jillian, let's each drink a soda and have a burping contest."

"Why?" she asked.

"Because I want to be better than you at something!" I said.

I downed my soda. She downed hers.

"Let the burping begin!" I said.

 Here's how hers turned out:

Here's how mine turned out:

"Booyah!" I said to Jillian. "Call me Burper King. Home of the Whopper!" I gave my booyah bootie a shake.

3

Hip to the Hop

Mrs. Sippy and I set our cupcakes and signs on a picnic table in the park. The sun was shining. The sky was blue. People were jogging, pushing strollers, and walking along the path.

"Cupcakes! Won't you please buy our cupcakes?" Jillian called out in her old lady voice. "Cupcakes for a good cause!"

"Your old lady voice is too soft,"

I said. "We need some major boom. Some snap, crackle, and pop to get this party started."

I grabbed two sticks, gave them to Jillian, and told her to drum a *boom-boom* beat on the table.

"Why?" she asked.

"Jillian," I said, "just go with the flow. Ride with the tide. Move with the groove. Float with the boat. Run with the fun. Dance with the chance. Pound with the sound. Hop with the pop."

"But I'm not a go-with-the-flow kind of person," she said.

I sighed. Sometimes you've got to do it all yourself. I started beat boxing, going, *"Boom. Boom. Boom diddy boom."*

That beat went straight to my feet, and I started hip-hopping with my big bottom. Old ladies hip-hopping with big bottoms make people stop and notice.

Within minutes, we had a crowd. Jillian finally got the idea and pounded out a beat on the table.

Boom. Boom. Boom diddy boom.

My flow was coming on. I got my old lady voice going, and I started to rap:

"One for the money,
two for the show,
three for the doggies,
and here we go.
I'm gonna get in your grill
till you spill some bills
'cause the doggy shelter
needs food and pills.
Get your cup! Get your cake!
Eat it up! You can make
a mutt ruff with this stuff.
One buck's not enough.
Be a friend—that's waz up.
Show some love to a pup!"

The crowd went wild.

"Go, Grandma! I'll take a
cupcake!" a woman called out.

"Me, too!" a man said. "I'll add

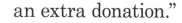
an extra donation."

"I'll take six!"
another woman said.

Jillian and I grinned.

Oooh, it felt good to
be doing a good deed.
Indeed.

I kept my *boom-boom* going. We
sold all of Jillian's cupcakes and got
tons of extra donations.

"If you had used a recipe," Jillian
said, "we could have sold yours, too."

I was starting to feel a little sad
when a guy walked up with his dog on
a leash. The dog lunged straight for
my so-called cupcakes.

"No, Maxer!" the guy called,
pulling on the dog's leash.

"It's the bacon," I said. "Everything

is better with bacon." I threw the dog one of my treats, and he gobbled it right up.

That gave me a great idea.

I took the sticks and got a beat going.

I held up one of my ugly cupcakes and started to rap:

"One for the money,
      two for the show,
      three for the doggies,
      and here we go.
See these yucky yucks?
Look like they're made of muck,
      hard as hockey pucks?
Well, it's your lucky day

'cause I'm here to say
that they're not your eats.
They're doggy treats!
So buy a li'l chow-chow
for your li'l bowwow.
We'll donate all the dough
to the shelter now."

Mrs. Sippy's bootie wasn't as big as mine, but she got it shaking, too. And the crowd loved it.

"I'll buy some dog biscuits!" a guy said.

"Me, too!" someone else said.

We sold all but two of my yucky-cakes. I put the leftovers in my dress pocket, and Jillian put all the money into her purse. Then we did a li'l hip-hop to celebrate:

"We be makin' bacon,
    showin' love to the pups.
Gonna give up the money,
    say ruff ruff ruff."

4

Punked

"We did a good job, Billy!" Jillian said as we walked to the shelter. "This money will buy a lot of food and medicine for the dogs."

"And we earned it, dude!" I said. "Let's go get a bacon burger!" I started doing my dance moves down the street.

"I feel good, too," Jillian said. "But let's get this money to the shelter right now." She started speed-walking. The shelter was about six blocks away, on a quiet street.

When we were almost at the shelter, I saw two guys getting out of a parked car. "Oops. Slow down and look old, Mrs. Sippy," I said.

When you're excited, it's hard to remember that you're eighty years old.

The two men strolled toward us. As we passed, I said, "Lovely day, isn't it?"

One man smiled and said, "Yes."

The other one grabbed Jillian's purse! They were muggers!

"Hey!" Jillian cried.

The crook started to run down an alley. I ran after him and tripped. Yep. Shouldn't have worn my heels.

"That's our money!" I cried. "Give it back."

The man stopped, turned around, and took off his beard and hat. It was Tanya Crook, aka Mom.

Dad was right behind us. He laughed and pulled off his mustache and glasses. "You guys just got punked!"

"Mom! Dad!" Jillian said. "What are you doing here?"

"We were driving around, looking for the next store to rob, when we saw you two," Mom said. "We decided to see if you were on your toes. You know there are crooks in this world."

"Yeah, and you guys just got hit." Dad opened Jillian's purse. "Wow! That's a lot of cash! What were you guys doing?"

Jillian and I looked at each other.

"Uh-uh-umm," I stammered.

Mom took the purse and pulled out the Lucky Dog Shelter flyer.

"Were you going to buy a dog?" Dad asked.

"I've always wanted a dog," I said. It was true.

"A Crook would never *buy* a dog, Billy," Mom said.

"Yeah," Dad said. "If you want a dog, *steal* it."

Mom tore up the flyer. "And don't steal a mutt from a shelter. Steal a really high-class dog."

"Yeah," Dad said. "Steal the best. Come on. We'll give you a ride home and help you come up with a plan."

Mom put her beard back on. Dad put his mustache back on. The four of us walked back to the car.

I thought about all those poor hungry dogs at the shelter.

No high-fiving huskies.

No dancing Dalmations.

No cheering Chihuahuas.

No bunny-hopping basset hounds.

I looked at Jillian. She looked sad, too. I felt like crying. My stomach growled. Sad, and hungry, too. Dude. It was not my day. What I'd give for a bacon burg—

Wait a minute. I pulled a doggy treat out of my pocket and sniffed it.

Yum. Bacon.

Jillian looked at me. "You're not going to eat that, are you?"

I took a nibble. It tasted like . . . *rotten tree bark.*

"Bad, huh?" Jillian asked.

I smiled and popped the whole thing in my mouth anyway. That's how I roll.

5

Oodles of Poodles

"By the way," Mom said from the front seat. "We stopped at Beggin' fer Burgers. Here." She handed a bag to us in the backseat. Bacon cheeseburgers!

"Why didn't you tell me before?" I asked.

I ate two. I wanted to eat another, but I was too full. So I put it in my pocket for later.

"I have an idea, Tanya," Dad said

as he was driving us home. "Let's steal a dog from the Poodle Palace."

"Nice idea," Mom said. "That's where all the rich people take their dogs to get haircuts. We can steal a dog with style."

Jillian and I looked at each other. Uh-oh.

"It might not be a great idea to steal somebody else's dog," Jillian blurted out. "The owners would be sad."

Mom and Dad looked horrified. Crooks don't care about other people's feelings.

"Ha-ha-ha!" I laughed. "That was a good one, Jillian!"

Mom and Dad laughed. Jillian gave me a secret thumbs-up.

"Let's do it now," Dad said. "Why wait?" He turned right, heading toward Michigan Avenue.

"When we get there, you two hop out," Mom said. "Pretend you're dog owners looking for a new pet salon. No one will suspect two old ladies of being dog robbers. Billy, say something to make everyone look at you. Jillian, when everyone is looking at Billy, grab the dog, make a run for it, and hop in the car. We'll be waiting."

"It's a plan!" Dad said, and turned onto Michigan Avenue. We passed a jewelry shop, a fancy clothes store, and a restaurant.

"People who shop here sure are rich!" Dad said. He pulled over at the Poodle Palace.

Through the window we could see oodles of poodles sitting on red velvet cushions, getting haircuts and shampoos.

"Go for it, kids!" Mom said.

Jillian and I got out. Slowly, we walked toward the doors.

"Once we're inside the salon," Jillian whispered, "say something to get everyone to look at you, like Mom

said. I'll pick up a dog that's being
shampooed, but then I'll pretend it's
too slippery to hold. I'll let go of the
dog, and we'll race back to the car.
I'll tell Mom and Dad we just couldn't
pull it off. "

"Got it!" I said.

"Are you sure?" Jillian asked.

"Yep." I nodded.

We walked in.

Jillian looked at me.

I froze. My mind went blank.

"Say something to make
everybody look at you," Jillian
whispered. "Mom and Dad are
watching."

I said what crooks usually say to
a lot of rich-looking people. "Hello," I
said. "This is a stickup!"

A woman screamed and dropped her dog brush. Two poodles fainted.

I didn't know what to do. I reached into my pocket and pulled out my . . . bacon cheeseburger.

"Yip!" A cute white poodle jumped off her red velvet pillow and headed straight toward me.

I turned and ran.

The poodle was on my heels.

Jillian ran, too.

"Throw the burger down!" Jillian said.

I yelled, "Why would I ever want to throw away a bacon cheeseburger?"

We hopped into the car. The poodle hopped right into my lap and started eating my cheeseburger.

Oh. That's why.

Dad took off.

"Great job, Billy!" Mom and Dad said.

"Yeah," Jillian said. "Great job, Billy."

"Well," I said, "at least we got a dog with good taste."

6

Diary of a Wimpy Dog

Sniff. Sniff. The poodle sniffed our feet. Jillian and I were back in our kitchen, wearing our kid clothes. Our parents were out stealing dog food and a leash.

"We have to get this poodle back to her owner," Jillian said. "It isn't right to steal someone's dog!"

I was about to agree when I felt gas gurgling in my tummy. Those doggy treats mixed with the bacon

cheeseburgers were making me want
to burp.

"We also have to get that money
to the shelter," Jillian went on. "It
wouldn't be fair to keep it."

The gas was moving up the
pipeline. A major burp was on its way
north. I couldn't help it. *"UUURP!"*
I let out a huge bacon-flavored burp
right in her face.

LITTLE QUIZ

You know your burp is bad when:

a) You knock your sister over.

b) You knock a dog over.

c) You have to plug your own nose.

d) All of the above.

The correct answer is *d*, all of the above.

Whew!

Jillian got up. "That gives me an idea!"

"We keep burping until the dog wants to run away?" I asked.

"No," Jillian said. "But dogs do have a very good sense of smell. I bet

42

if we let her out, she'll run right back to her owner. We can tell Mom and Dad the bad news. Then we can sneak out and deliver the cupcake money to the shelter."

"I like the burping idea. But we can give yours a try." I opened the front door. "Go home, doggy."

The dog rolled over and played dead. Give a dog a chance, and what do you get? Nothing. Nada. Zero. Zip.

"Yo, dawg!" I got down on my knees and looked at the panting poodle. "Stop smiling. I have something important to tell you."

"Yip." The poodle smiled.

"Dawg! This is serious! You have been stolen!"

"Yip," the poodle said.

"Listen to me, you wacko mutt!" I said. "You have to run back to your owner." I pointed to the door. "Scram!"

She sat up on her hind legs.

"Don't sit! Run. Go *zoom-zoom*. Put your paws on the pavement. Make like a banana and split," I said.

She rolled over and played deader.

I pulled my last doggy treat out of my pocket and ran out the door. It was a risk since I wasn't in disguise. I crouched down and held out the treat. "Here, dawg! Hurry! Come get the treat!"

The dog looked at me.

"It's got bacon in it."

The dog trotted to the doorway.

"Come on, girl!" I waved the treat

in the air to send the bacon smell out.

Sniff. Sniff. The dog trotted over and gobbled up the treat.

"Now, go home!"

She looked in my face and . . . *"Aaachoo!"*

SOME INTERESTING FACTS ABOUT DOGS

1. Dogs sneeze.
2. Dogs have snot.

3. Dog snot is wet.
4. Dog snot is slimy.
5. Dog snot smells like worms mixed with bacon.
6. Dog snot tastes like worm guts mixed with hummus and bacon.
7. If you remove the dog snot from your face by wiping it on your sister's face, she will get mad.

"Look," Jillian said. "A squirrel! Dogs love to chase squirrels. Come on, girl! Go chase that squirrel."

The squirrel looked at the dog. The dog looked at the squirrel.

And then the li'l wimp ran inside.

"Heee-heee-hee!" The squirrel laughed his head off.

A couple of his squirrely friends

came over to his branch to see what was up. They were probably thinking, *That dog is a chicken!*

Jillian and I went inside.

"We need a new plan, Billy," Jillian said.

"I have an idea," I said. "Let's get the mutt to do something bad. Then Mom and Dad will want to get rid of her."

"Great idea!" Jillian said.

I got Dad's favorite slipper. "Come on, dawg. Chew it up!"

The poodle sniffed it. Then she sneezed in my face.

AN INTERESTING FACT ABOUT ME

1. I do not learn from my mistakes.

After I wiped the dog snot off my face, Jillian said, "Show her what you mean."

I got on my hands and knees. "Yip. Yip," I said. "Watch me." I chomped down on Dad's slipper. "*Chomp. Chomp. Blech.*" I spit it out. "Dad's feet stink."

Jillian jumped back. "Don't barf!"

"Hey, dogs barf all the time." I grabbed my mom's favorite coat. "Come on, dawg. Barf on this coat."

The poodle looked at me like I was insane.

"Go like this." I pretended to barf all over my mom's coat.

Guess what happened next? The dog rolled over and went belly up again.

"I know what to get this dog for her birthday," I told Jillian.

"What?" Jillian asked.

"A gravestone," I said. "Playing dead is the only thing she likes to do."

I looked at the dog. "Enough with the zombie stuff," I said. "Do something!"

The dog trotted over to the couch, hopped up, hit the remote control with her paw, and turned on the TV.

"Yip. Yip," she said with a smile.

"Great," I said. "Our parents kidnapped a couch potato."

7

Poochie Smoochie

"Look, Billy!" Jillian said. "The dog turned on *The Poochie Smoochie Show.*"

"Jillian," I said, "this is not a time to watch TV."

"No. Look!" She pointed.

The Poochie Smoochie Show was just starting. The star of the show, a cute white poodle, was trotting down a busy street—

Wait a minute. The dog in our

living room looked like the dog on TV.

Jillian grabbed my arm. "Do you think we stole Poochie Smoochie?"

"Yip." The dog on TV yipped.

"Yip." The dog in our living room yipped.

Just then the TV show cut off and a TV news reporter came on.

"Breaking news," the announcer said. "Poochie Smoochie, the rich and famous TV dog, was at her favorite doggy salon when two women broke in and kidnapped her. Police are on the lookout for these suspects. . . ."

Some bad video footage of us walking into the Poodle Palace flashed on the screen. The Poodle Palace must have a hidden camera.

"We've got a problem," Jillian said.

"I know, right? We are way cuter than that," I said.

"No. We stole the richest and most famous dog in the whole country. We have to take her back!"

"I have an idea," I said. "What is Poochie really good at?"

"Playing dead?" she guessed.

"Yep," I said. "We'll get Poochie to play dead and we'll pretend to bury her. Then we'll sneak her out and return her."

"I don't know . . . ," Jillian said.

We heard the sound of Ron and Tanya's car in the driveway.

I grabbed my video camera and showed it to Poochie. "Time to act. It's *The Poochie Smoochie Show.* Poochie, when I say 'action,' I want you to play dead."

Poochie nodded.

"Action," I whispered.

That dog fell over like a rock!

My parents walked in.

Poochie didn't move.

"What's going on?" Mom asked.

"I think the dog had a heart

attack," I said. "We were playing with her . . . and she . . . she . . ."

Jillian took off her hoodie and put it over Poochie.

"Poor, poor Poo—poodle." I sniffed. "She bit the dust. She cashed out. She chewed on her last bone. She's on a permanent vacation. She's done like dinner. She went to yip with the angels. She's gone to that great Poodle Party in the sky." Big, fat tears rolled down my cheeks. "You were too young to die, poodle."

It was an amazing performance! I was fantastic! I could get a job in Hollywood!

"Just our luck to get a bum dog," Dad said.

"Yeah. Great," Mom said. "Now

what do we do with all this dog food?"

"Billy will eat it," Jillian said. She couldn't resist.

I, however, stayed in character. I sniffed. "How can you joke at a time like this?"

She hid her grin. "I'm sorry, Billy. You're right. This is a sad day. Let's give this dog a funeral."

"Okay, Jillian." I scooped up the lifeless dog in my arms and carried her into the backyard. Poochie was doing great.

Jillian got a shovel and began digging a hole.

Our parents watched from the doorway.

Jillian glanced at me and whispered, "Just bend over and

pretend to put her in the hole. I'll go
in and distract them, then you can
hide Poochie in the garage."

"Got it," I whispered.

We were a team.

In a loud voice, I began the
funeral. "Dearly beloved," I said, "we
are gathered here today to say good-
bye to our four-legged friend."

I heard a noise in the tree above
me. Oh, no! A squirrel!

Poochie opened one eye. And then the other.

Be brave, Poochie, I thought. *Make like a corpse and stay dead.*

"This poor poodle has truly died," I said loudly. "Never to yip or yap again."

"Hee-hee-hee!" The squirrel jumped to a lower branch.

Don't move, Poochie. Don't let that squirrel get to y—

"Yip." Poochie leaped out of my arms, ran into the house, and jumped into my dad's arms.

Mom and Dad looked at me for an explanation.

"She's alive!" I yelled. "It's a miracle!"

8

What's Worse than Worst?

*S*niff. *Sniff. Sniff.*

Jillian and I were in her room, plotting our next move. I was sitting on Jillian's bed, shoes and socks off, and Poochie was sniffing my toes.

Sniff. Sniff. Sniff.

Then, *Lick. Lick. Lick.*

"Finally, someone who appreciates the smell and taste of my ten little piggies," I said.

"That's disgusting," Jillian said.

"You're just jealous," I said. "My toes taste better than yours."

"Get serious. The cops are on the lookout." Jillian was nervous. "We can't use our Mrs. Sippy or Mrs. Whiffbacon disguises again."

"No problemo," I said. "We have lots of disguises."

She still looked nervous. "But even if we're wearing a new disguise, we can't walk out with Poochie or someone will recognize her and call the cops."

"We could disguise Poochie," I said.

Poochie stopped licking my toes and said, "Yip." I think she liked that idea almost as much as my toes.

"We'll disguise Poochie," I

explained. "Then we'll put her in a bag with a note that says 'I'm Poochie Smoochie.' We'll secretly drop her off at the salon. The salon lady will return Poochie to her owner."

"Not bad," Jillian said. "You work on the dog disguise. I'm going to spy on Mom and Dad. If they find out that we have the rich and famous Poochie Smoochie, things might get worse."

She took out two mini-flashlights and handed me one.

"What do I need a flashlight for?" I asked.

"It's not a flashlight. It's my new invention called the Buzzer." She pushed a button on her flashlight.

Bzz! Mine gave my hand a zap, sort of like a mosquito bite. "Ouch."

"It's a signal," she said. "If you feel it, I need you to come and help me."

I rubbed my hand. "Why did you have to make it zap?" I asked.

She gave me a look. "To get your attention," she said. "If you need me, press the button on yours."

"Like this?" I pushed my Buzzer button.

Bzz! She jumped.

"Well, it works," I said.

"Speaking of work," she said, "get going on that dog disguise." She took off.

Five, four, three, two, one. I pushed my Buzzer button.

She ran back in. "What is it?"

"I'm hungry," I said.

"The Buzzer is for emergencies, Billy," she said.

"But Poochie ate my last bacon cheeseburger," I said.

"Tell your tummy to get over it," she said, and walked out.

I looked at Poochie. "You understand me, don't you, dawg?"

"Yip," she said, and licked my toes.

"All right. I know you love my toes, but it's time to try out some canine costumes."

DOGGY DISGUISES

Punk Poochie

Skunk Poochie

Poochie Rabbit

Poochie, Pirate of the Caribbean

Poochie Red Riding Hood

Poochie Gucci

I was trying to decide which disguise was the best when . . . *bzz!* Something stung me.

It was annoying.

"Poochie, did you bring fleas into this house?" I asked. "Something just bit me."

Poochie tilted her head.

Bzz!

"Yeow!" It stung me again.

Oh . . . the Buzzer.

I put Poochie in the Gucci and I tiptoed downstairs. *Tip. Tip. Tip.*

Jillian was by the door to the living room. She waved me over. "Hurry—things just got worse," she whispered. "Mom heard the news about Poochie on the TV. I tried to interrupt, but it was too late."

We put our ears to the door. It sounded like Mom was making a phone call.

"I've got the number right, Ron,"

Mom said. "I just dialed. Now, be quiet. Hello, is this the owner of Poochie Smoochie?" Mom was using a fake voice, low and gruff. "We have your dog, and you'll have to pay us a big ransom to get her back."

Dognapping! Jillian and I looked at each other. Why couldn't Ron

and Tanya just use the phone to do something good for the world—like returning a poor dog to her rightful owner or ordering me a pizza with bacon?

"That's right," Mom said. "We're the dognappers. Put ten thousand dollars in a suitcase and drop it near the fountain in Higgins Park at midnight tonight. Or else."

Poochie stuck her head out of the purse, as if she wanted to hear what was going on.

"And no cops. Got it?" Mom said, and then she ended the call.

"Hot diggety," Dad said.

"There's only one problem, Ron. Dogs have a great sense of smell. What if we give the dog back and they use it to track us down?"

"Easy peasy. We don't give the dog back," Dad said. "We drop Poochie off in a field somewhere. Then we give her owner a box with a brick in it. We take the money and run. Poochie will love living by herself in the country."

Jillian and I looked at Poochie in the Gucci. Poochie Smoochie, living in a field, with no velvet pillow, no shampoo, no TV?

"The kids don't have to know," Mom said. "We'll all go to bed early and then we can sneak out, get rid of the dog, and pick up the dough."

"Yeah. We'll tell the kids that Poochie ran away." Dad chuckled.

Jillian and I looked at each other.

How could we get Poochie back to her owner?

"Come on, Ron. Let's get everything ready," Mom said.

Jillian grabbed my arm, and we ran into the kitchen.

"What should we do?" Jillian whispered.

"Make bacon cupcakes," I whispered.

"How is that going to help Poochie?" Jillian whispered.

"It won't, but it'll make our taste buds happy."

"Forget it," Jillian said. "I can't bake at a time like this."

I set the Gucci purse down. Poochie hopped out and went straight for my toes.

Lick. Lick. Lick.

I wiggled my toes and smiled at Jillian. "At least somebody's taste buds are happy."

9

Midnight Madness

It's hard to enjoy a good toe-licking when you know that the dog you accidentally stole is headed for a life of meadow-fresh misery.

Jillian and I didn't even have time to plan. It was a Wednesday, and after dinner on Wednesdays, we have lessons. We're homeschooled. Tonight, we were having a test: break into a second-story window without a ladder. Jillian went first. She had invented a ninja grappling hook and ninja shoes with sticky soles. She had practiced. She passed the test.

My turn.

WHAT HAPPENS IF YOU DON'T PRACTICE

← 1. Instead of throwing the ninja grappling hook over the roof, you throw it *through* the window.

← 2. Instead of wearing the ninja shoes with the sticky soles, you wear your flip-flops with the slippery soles.

← 3. When you finally make it up to the window, you look down.

"Billy," Mom said.

"I know. I didn't do my homework," I said. "Sorry."

Dad yawned. "Boy, oh, boy, I'm tired."

Mom yawned. "Me, too. I think we should all go to bed early tonight. Even Poochie looks tired, right, Poochie?"

"Yip," Poochie said.

"We made a nice bed for Poochie in our room, didn't we, Ron?" Mom said.

Dad nodded. "A nice, cozy bed."

Jillian and I traded looks. We still didn't have a plan.

We all went to bed. After a few minutes, I heard Mom and Dad sneak out with Poochie.

Poor Poochie. Jillian and I had to do something, but what?

Suddenly . . . *bzz!*

Something bit my toe. *Yeow!* Bedbugs? I got out of bed and started slapping my sheet. I slapped something hard. *Bzz!*

Yeow! It got my hand. *That must be one giant bedbug*, I thought.

I picked up my baseball bat and was about to smash it.

Jillian walked in. "What are you doing?"

"Killing giant bedbugs," I said.

Jillian grabbed the bat, whipped off my sheet, and picked up the Buzzer. "I put it here so I could signal you when the coast was clear to come to my room."

"Oh," I said. "One of these days, I'm going to remember that thing."

"We need to save Poochie," Jillian said.

"I agree," I said. "But how?"

"We could give Mom and Dad a taste of their own medicine," she said.

"I don't think Mom and Dad are taking any medicine."

"*No.* That's not what I mean," Jillian said. "What I mean is we could steal the dog from them before they have a chance to do anything."

So we put on our secret Crook uniforms—black turtlenecks and our sneaky black caps. Jillian grabbed her favorite tools and the money we'd collected for the shelter, just in case we needed it.

"Let's hurry," I said. "We have to get to Higgins Park, wherever that is. That's where they told Poochie's owner to drop the money."

"They're not going to the park yet," Jillian said. "We have to get to Gregory Street first."

"Why?"

She showed me a map on her smartphone. "I put a tracking device on Poochie Smoochie's collar. I can track her with my phone. See the

small blinking white dot? That's Poochie. They're headed down Gregory Street toward Elm Avenue right now."

"That's amazing!" I exclaimed.

Jillian grinned. "You mean I'm amazing?"

"No, what's amazing is that there's a Beggin' fer Burgers on Gregory Street!" I said. "On the way, we could—"

Jillian stopped me. "We're not stopping at Beggin' fer Burgers."

"How did you know what I was about to say?"

"Whenever you think about bacon, you get this crazy look in your eyes," Jillian said. "Put that craving on hold. Let's go."

10

Choo Choo Uh-Oh

Jillian pulled me toward the garage.

"But Mom and Dad took the van," I said. "We can't pedal our bikes fast enough to catch up."

Jillian opened the door and turned on the light. She ran over and pulled two objects out of a box. "It's time to test out my new inventions."

"Backpacks?"

"Jetpacks." She grinned. "They look like backpacks, but they have a secret jetpack hidden inside." She strapped one on my back. "With this, you won't even need to pedal."

I hopped on my bike.

"Wait," Jillian said. "Let's talk through our plan first."

"Just tell me how to start," I said.

"You start the motor by pulling on the string," she said. "And you stop it by—"

I couldn't wait. I pulled on the string. *Yank!*

VROOOM!

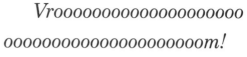

*Vroooooooooooooooooooooo
ooooooooooooooooooooooom!*

I blasted right through
the garage door and was
off.

"Whoaaaaaaa!" I
held on tight. The night
was black. No moon. Dark houses
and trees flashed by. I turned onto
Gregory Street. Beggin' fer Burgers
was still open. *Vroom* . . . Beggin' fer
Burgers was a blur. *Noooooo!*

I glanced behind. Jillian was
catching up to me.

"Billy!"

I tried to slow down, but the
jetpack seemed to have only one
speed.

"Turn right at the next street," she

called out to me. "Then left. Then go straight. They're heading toward the train tracks."

I *vroomed*. Right. Left. Straight. A gas station . . . a car dealership . . . and then nothing but dark fields. A lonesome road. After a few seconds, I could see two red taillights ahead. I figured it must be Mom and Dad's van. We were catching up to them. I needed to slow down.

I pulled the string again, but that just made the jetpack go faster.

Ahead, one lone street lamp showed a train signal.

Right before the train tracks, the van turned left into a cornfield.

Vroom! I zipped right by the cornfield turnoff and raced over the train track. Well, at least I was going too fast to be seen. Jillian sped up until she was next to me.

"You have to stop slowly. Press the button on your left shoulder strap gently and hold it down." She pressed her button and began to slow down.

I reached up and pushed my button hard. *ERRR!*

Instead of slowing down, my jetpack stopped completely. My bike flew out from under me. I did a backward flip in the air and landed in a bush.

Jillian parked her bike while I

untangled myself from the bush.

I rubbed my rear end and wished I had some of Mrs. Whiffbacon's padding. "Where is the Whopper when you need it?" I asked.

"We have to sneak back and steal Poochie," Jillian said. "Come on."

We walked our bikes back toward the train tracks. An old barn was

there, and we peered out from behind it toward the cornfield. The sound of a train whistle came from the distance.

"They're getting out of the van," Jillian whispered.

Just over the tracks, we could see Mom and Dad in the glow from the street lamp. Dad had Poochie in his arms.

"Let's make it quick," Mom said. "Whoever just zipped by on those motorcycles might be coming back."

Dad set Poochie down. "There you go, girl. Run and play!"

"Yip. Yip." Poochie sat on her hind legs.

Dad pointed to the field. "Take your paws and scram!"

Poochie licked her paws.

"Come on, Ron," Mom said. "Let's get out of here."

"Yeah, let's go get that ransom money," Dad said. They hopped in the van and drove off.

Poochie sat there, sniffing the air, looking lost and sad.

"Hey, Poochie," I called. "Come here."

"Oh, no!" Jillian pointed to the light down the track. "The train is coming!"

"Come quick, Poochie!" I said, clapping my hands.

Poochie walked onto the tracks, rolled over, and played dead.

"Nooooo!" I shouted. "That is not the place to play dead!"

Choo. Choo. The train was coming! I started running toward the track.

The light was bright. The engine was seconds away.

"Watch out!" Jillian yelled. She

pulled out her ninja net and tossed it
toward the track.

I ducked.

Choo. Choo.

The net sailed over me and landed
on Poochie. I jumped up and grabbed
the rope to the net. We both yanked
on it and . . .

Whooooooooosh. Poochie toppled
off the tracks, just as the train
whizzed by.

"We did it!" Jillian cried.

We ran and opened the net.

A very happy Poochie face looked
up at us. "Yip! Yip! Yippee!" She
licked our faces, her round, dark
eyes glittering. Even without a bacon
cheeseburger in me, my insides were
feeling all warm and delicious.

Jillian started jumping up and down with joy. "We are mad crazy do-gooders!" Jillian said.

Yep. That's how we roll.

11

It's a Bird. It's a Plane. It's a Burger?

"Come on," Jillian said. "We saved Poochie. Now we have to get her back to her owner and stop Mom and Dad from collecting the ransom."

"To Higgins Park!" I put Poochie in my backpack and we hopped on our bikes.

I pulled the string! *Vroom!*

"Not so fast!" Jillian called out.

I pushed the slow-down button. Jillian knew the way, so I followed her. As we turned onto Gregory Street, I called up, "Now can we stop at Beggin' fer Burgers?"

"No."

"But I need some cheering up, and nothing says cheer better than a bacon cheeseburger," I yelled.

"Why do you need cheering up?" she called back. "We saved Poochie."

"*You* saved Poochie. I haven't done anything yet but chew on Dad's slipper and fall on my rump."

"We're a team," Jillian called back. "And it's not over yet. We're almost there. Watch out!"

Jillian turned onto Higgins Street. I saw the sign for the park ahead.

SNIFF SNIFF SNIFF SNIFF

Just across
the street from the
park was the glow
of . . . guess what?
Another Beggin'
fer Burgers sign!
The smell of burgers zoomed right up
my nostrils.

"Yip." Poochie stuck her head out
of the backpack.

Jillian saw it, too. "All right. Go
for it, but make it quick."

I made a quick turn into the drive-
through.

"One bacon cheeseburger," I said.
"Please make it snappy."

I paid, grabbed the bag, stuffed it down my jacket, and *vroomed* back to the street.

Jillian was waiting for me by the entrance to the park. "Eat it later. We've got to go find Poochie's owner."

We parked our bikes behind a tree.

As soon as I took Poochie out of my backpack, she was all up in my jacket, sniffing her brains out. That bacon cheeseburger aroma is hard to resist. "Jillian says we got to hurry," I whispered, and set her down on the ground.

"Hold tight to her leash," Jillian said. "And we have to stay in the shadows so Mom and Dad don't see us. I'm sure they're already here somewhere."

I held on tight to Poochie's leash, and we crept through the park.

"I can see the lights of the fountain this way," Jillian whispered, heading toward the right.

Poochie started pulling left, toward a tree by the playground.

"This way!" Jillian whispered.

Poochie kept pulling toward that tree. "I think she needs to go!" I whispered. "You know, to do what dogs do outside."

"Now?" Jillian whispered.

"When you got to go, you got to go," I said as Poochie pulled me over.

The playground had a very cool twisty slide. While Poochie was sniffing around, deciding where to drop her doo-doo, I decided to go down the slide. I climbed up the steps.

"Not now, Billy," Jillian whispered.

"This is too cool to pass up," I said as I sat at the top.

Poochie trotted over and sniffed the bottom of the slide.

"Oh, no, you don't," I said. "Get away from there."

She hopped up on the slide and looked at me.

"Go under a tree like a normal dog, you crazy mutt!" I said.

She squatted.

"Nooooooooo!" I waved and lost my grip on the slide. *Zooooom!* Down I went. I slid around and around, getting a glimpse of the gift Poochie had left at the bottom. "Nooooooo!" At the last second I pulled my knees up, pushed off, and did a flying somersault over the poop.

Whew!

"Yip," Poochie said.

"Yuck," I said. "You need some manners, mutt!"

Jillian and I both looked at the mess. "We can't just leave this here," she said. "Some poor kindergartner is going to get slimed."

I found a big leaf. Then I plugged my nose, scooped up the poop with the leaf, and put it under a nearby bush. Oh, the joy of having a dog!

"Shh!" Jillian said. "I hear something."

We followed the noise. As we turned a corner, we could see the whole fountain, lit from below. We hid in the shadows.

"Look." I pointed. Our van was parked on the road, just beyond the fountain. Our parents were wearing disguises to look like park employees. Mom was in the driver's seat. Dad was waiting in front of the van with a box.

"That's the box with the brick," Jillian whispered.

They had fake license plates on the van. Ron and Tanya Crook had thought of everything.

Lights flashed and then a car

pulled up. It was a limousine. It had
to be the rich owner!

A woman got out with a suitcase.

Dad stayed by the van. "Try any
funny business, and your dog is dead!"
he said.

The woman held out the suitcase.
"It's all here. Just give me the dog."

Jillian crouched down. "Poochie,"
she whispered, "run to your owner!
Now!"

Poochie rolled over and played dead.

I knew what I had to do. I pulled out the delicious bacon cheeseburger. Poochie jumped up.

I let her sniff it once and then I pulled it back, winding up for the pitch. I threw that sucker as hard as I could. It went flying over the fountain.

"Yip!" Poochie went chasing after it.

The bun fell off, but the cheese held the bacon to the burger and it sailed in a long, beautiful arc and then hit the side of the limo with a

smack! Poochie was on it in a second.

"Poochie!" the owner cried with joy.

"Poochie?" Dad exclaimed. He looked around, wondering what had happened, and we ducked back into the shadows.

Jillian pulled out her smartphone and hit the sound button. A fake siren wailed. She turned up the volume.

I peeked out and saw Dad running for the van. He thought the cops were coming. With a squeal of tires, the van was gone.

"We did it!" Jillian and I jumped up and started dancing around.

"Great job with the burger, Billy!" Jillian said.

"Nice touch with the siren, Jillian," I said.

I was so happy, I got my *boom-boom* going.

*"One for the money,
two for the show,
three for the doggies,
and here we go."*

The owner heard and came running over with Poochie in her arms. "Did you throw that burger?"

I grinned, still holding the bag.

Jillian turned off the siren on her cell phone.

"You saved my dog!" the owner exclaimed. "I'd like to give you two kids a reward."

Jillian pulled the flyer for the shelter out of her pocket and handed it to the woman. "We're collecting money for the Lucky Dog Shelter," she said. "So the dogs will have enough food and medicine."

"What a wonderful idea," the woman said. She handed over the suitcase. "Please take this money."

We gulped.

"I was going to give it to some terrible crooks to get Poochie back," the woman said. "This is a much better cause."

"Thank you!" Jillian said.

"Yip!" said Poochie.

"Aw, what a cute dog," Jillian said. "Can we pet her?"

The owner set Poochie down, and we each gave her a hug. I was going to miss that squirrel-hating, dead-playing, toe-licking, bacon-loving mutt.

12

Tip Tip Squish

The street was dark. The door was locked. I was using Jillian's lock opener to break into the Lucky Dog Shelter.

Most crooks break into a joint in order to steal some cash. Jillian and I were breaking in to *leave* some cash. Ron and Tanya would be horrified.

The lock popped, and I pushed the door open. "We're in," I said.

We slipped through the door,

tiptoed to the front desk, and put all the money there. Ten thousand dollars plus the money we'd collected from our bake sale.

The people who worked there were going to be so happy.

Jillian pulled my arm and pointed to a doorway marked DOGS.

"Are you thinking what I'm thinking?" I asked.

She grinned and nodded. "How could we come to a shelter and not play with the dogs?"

GAMES TO PLAY WITH DOGS AT ONE A.M.

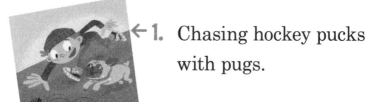 ← 1. Chasing hockey pucks with pugs.

2. Basketball with beagles.

3. Shuffleboard with → shih tzus.

← 4. Crack-the-whip with collies.

5. Drop-kicking with → dachshunds.

← 6. Hide-and-seek with Saint Bernards.

7. Follow-the-leader → with Labradors.

• • •

It was hard to say good-bye, but we had to go. I took off my shoes and let a little terrier lick my toes. Then we slipped out of the shelter and locked the doors tight.

"That was fun, wasn't it?" Jillian asked.

"Mad crazy fun," I said. "And my toes are squeaky clean!"

We got on our bikes. The street was peaceful. It was one of those nights that you don't want to end. We rode home the slow, quiet way.

"Don't you think it's strange that we want to do good deeds?" Jillian asked as we pedaled.

"Very strange," I agreed.

"After all, our parents hate to do

good deeds," Jillian added.

"Exactly," I said. "We're nuts."

Jillian whispered, "What if our parents are not really our parents?"

"That's insane, Jillian."

We turned the corner onto our street.

"But we're not anything like them," she said.

I looked at her. "If we're not Crooks, then who are we?"

"Mom and Dad are really good at stealing," she said.

"So?"

"So . . . maybe they stole us."

It was a crazy idea, but it kind of made sense.

"Maybe we're not even twins," I said.

"What makes you think that?"
Jillian asked.

"Because my toes taste better than yours."

She laughed.

"Okay. Seriously. When would they have stolen us?" I asked.

"When we were born!" Jillian said. "They could have stolen us from the hospital. I think we should go to that hospital and ask some questions."

"Let's go now," I whispered.

"Not now," Jillian said. "We have to act normal. Right now we need to get upstairs to our bedrooms without them seeing us. We can check out the hospital tomorrow."

We pulled into our driveway. The van was in the garage, and the light was on in the kitchen. We peeked in the window. Mom and Dad were having a midnight snack. For them, losing the ransom money was a big deal. No doubt they needed cheering up.

We tiptoed around the back and used the grappling hook to break into my room.

Those breaking-and-entering skills really come in handy when you need to break into your own house.

"Good night, Billy," Jillian whispered.

We gave each other a high five, and then she tiptoed off to her room.

I put on my pajamas and hopped into bed.

Just in time! A few minutes later,

Mom stuck her head in. I pretended to snore.

"He's asleep," I heard her whisper to Dad.

"Jillian is, too," Dad said.

I heard them tiptoe down the hall. *Tip. Tip. Tip.*

I kept wondering, had Ron and Tanya Crook stolen us? Were our real Dad and Mom out there somewhere, missing us? We would go to the hospital in the morning and look for clues. I figured the sooner I got to sleep, the sooner the morning would come.

I snuggled under my covers and wiggled my toes, which, by the way, had never been cleaner.

"Good night, Billy," I said to myself.

"But I'm too excited to sleep," I replied. "Please, sing me a lullaby."

"Oh, all right," I said to myself. "Just this once."

I got my *boom diddy boom* going and sang myself a li'l lullaby:

"See the stars in the sky?
Time for beddy-bye.
So be a good guy
*   and close your eyes.*
Give sleep a try
*   or I'll make a bacon pie*
*   and throw it in your face!"*

Mmm. Bacon pie. Now, that was something to dream about. Good night!

**Turn the page
for some
SECRET EXTRAS**

Secret Extras

You can share these ideas with your parents. Just don't show them to ours!

SECRET FACT

When we get hot, we sweat.
Dogs sweat, too, but not in the same places we do. Dogs sweat through the bottoms of their feet!

SECRET RIDDLE

How can you keep a dog from barking in the front yard?*

*Put the dog in the backyard.

SECRET GAME

The Poochie Smoochie Show

Use the stick puppets on pages 118–119 to create your own *Poochie Smoochie Show.*

- Make a copy of those pages or download the printable page on http: www.maryamato.com/secret-extras.
- Have a grown-up help cut out the puppets from your copy. Do not—we repeat, do not—cut them out of this book!
- Color them.

- Eat two Popsicles. Why? Because they're good . . . and because you need the sticks. Attach a Popsicle stick to the back of each puppet with tape.
- Make up a story about Poochie.
- Perform your show for your friends. If you don't have any friends, perform it for your grandma. If your grandma lives in Hong Kong, perform it for your dog. If your dog is asleep, perform it for the neighborhood squirrels. They will love it.

THE POOCHIE SMOOCHIE THEME SONG

Here's the theme song from *The Poochie Smoochie Show*. Start off your puppet show by singing this song loudly.

Look at Poo chie she's a cu tie walk ing down the street.

Hel lo Poo chie want some foo die? We'll give you a treat.

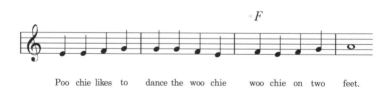

Poo chie likes to dance the woo chie woo chie on two feet.

Then she gives a smoo chie to ev ery one she meets.

By the way, dressing up pets in costumes can be fun for you but stressful for the pet, so if you want to dress up a pet, make some clothes for your Poochie stick puppet!

You can see some examples on http: www.maryamato.com/secret-extras.

MARY AMATO is an award-winning children's book author, poet, and songwriter whose novels have appeared on many state master lists. Her previous chapter books include the hilarious Riot Brothers series. She lives near Washington, DC. Visit her online at www.maryamato.com or follow her on Twitter @maryamato.

WARD JENKINS is an illustrator and animator. His previous books include the picture book *How to Train with a T. Rex and Win 8 Gold Medals*, by Michael Phelps with Alan Abrahamson. He lives in Portland, Oregon, with his wife and their two children. Visit him online at www.wardjenkins.com or follow him on Twitter @wardomatic.